A Packet of Seeds

Deborah Hopkinson

Pictures by

Bethanne Andersen

Greenwillow Books

An Imprint of HarperCollinsPublishers

For Vicki, Michael, and Sarah —D. H.

To those who know the healing
power of the earth —B. A.

A Packet of Seeds
Text copyright © 2004 by Deborah Hopkinson
Illustrations copyright © 2004 by Bethanne Andersen
All rights reserved. Manufactured in China
by South China Printing Company Ltd.
www.harpercollins.com
Gouache and oil paints were used to prepare the full-color art.
The text type is 14-point Horley Old Style.

Library of Congress Cataloging-in-Publication Data
Hopkinson, Deborah.
A packet of seeds / by Deborah Hopkinson ;
pictures by Bethanne Andersen.
  p. cm.
"Greenwillow Books."
Summary: When a pioneer family moves west, the mother misses
home so much that she will not even name the new baby until her
daughter thinks of just the right thing to cheer her up.
ISBN 0-06-009089-8 (trade). ISBN 0-06-009090-1 (lib. bdg.)
[1. Frontier and pioneer life—Fiction. 2. Homesickness—Fiction.
3. Gardens—Fiction. 4. Babies—Fiction.] I. Andersen,
Bethanne, (date), ill. II. Title.
PZ7.H78125Pac 2004 [E]—dc21 2003005489

First Edition 10 9 8 7 6 5

Greenwillow Books

MY pa was a man who dreamed of standing alone in an open field where the only shadow he could see was his own.

One day Pa came home with news about land to be had out west. I could tell he'd already made up his mind.

"Folks around here are getting close as kernels on a cob," he told Momma.

"But this is our home, James," Momma said. "My sister is here, and our friends."

All Pa could see was the new land before him. All Momma could feel was the sorrow of leaving everything behind.

But after that, Momma never said a word more. She just cooked and cleaned and packed to ready us for the long journey.

We left so early one morning, I didn't think anyone would come to say farewell. Then I heard the soft rustling of skirts.

Momma's friends gathered around in a circle. Each one kissed her, then pressed a small packet into her hand. Aunt Janice was last.

"Dear sister," she said, holding Momma tight. "I'm glad it's dawn so I can see your face just one more time."

My little brother, Jim, was already perched high on the wagon seat. The oxen moved in their traces and snorted in the chilly air.

Pa called out, "Mary, it's time."

Aunt Janice hugged me. "Take care of your momma, Annie."

Momma ducked her head and turned away without a word. I wondered if her voice was drowned by tears.

"This is it?" asked Momma, wiping the dust from her eyes. Our faces were burned and dry from the blazing sun. The animals stood thin and weary after so many weeks of walking.

Only Pa seemed as bright and cheerful as ever. "Mary, all this to the creek is ours!"

"It's so brown."

"Wait till spring, when we've cleared the land and planted our corn."

WE had a lot to do before winter set in. Pa made a simple sod
barn for our oxen and the cow. There was enough wood by the
creek, so Pa built us a rough cabin. And no matter how hard he
worked, Pa never seemed to lose heart.

"This cabin should keep us snug enough," he promised as
we patted mud into the cracks between the logs.

Our little cabin *was* strong. But nothing could keep out the
moaning of the wind. On winter nights, when the coyotes
howled near, a cold fear clung to me.

"Don't mind the coyotes, Annie. Why, they're the choir of
the prairies," our neighbor, Mrs. Johnston, told me.

But somehow I couldn't feel safe. Especially not with
Momma so still and sad.

I knew Momma wouldn't ask Pa to leave this new land.
She'd never give up and go home. But I wondered if I'd ever see
her smile again.

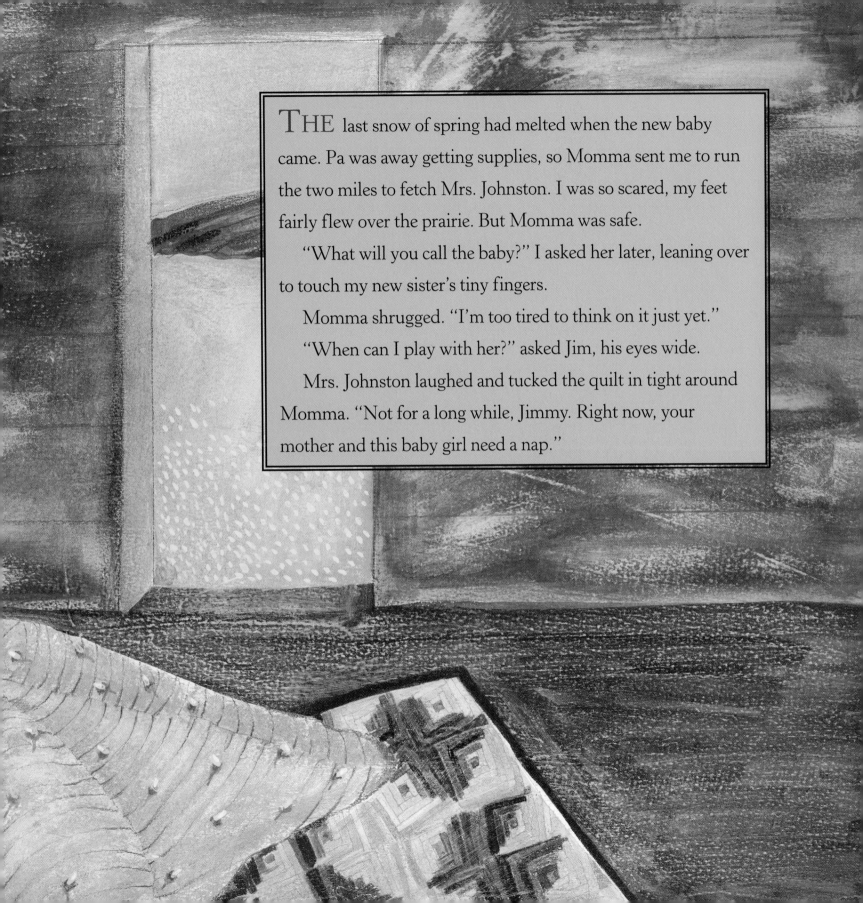

THE last snow of spring had melted when the new baby came. Pa was away getting supplies, so Momma sent me to run the two miles to fetch Mrs. Johnston. I was so scared, my feet fairly flew over the prairie. But Momma was safe.

"What will you call the baby?" I asked her later, leaning over to touch my new sister's tiny fingers.

Momma shrugged. "I'm too tired to think on it just yet."

"When can I play with her?" asked Jim, his eyes wide.

Mrs. Johnston laughed and tucked the quilt in tight around Momma. "Not for a long while, Jimmy. Right now, your mother and this baby girl need a nap."

While Momma slept, Mrs. Johnston helped me make biscuits.

"Anne, you must take special care of your mother just now," she said softly. "Her spirits seem low. And with a new baby . . ."

"I wish she could be happy here," I whispered.

Mrs. Johnston looked around us. The cabin floor was hard-packed dirt. Two small windows let in dim light. And the prairie wind never let up its wild, low whine.

"I expect she misses her old home. I know I do," said Mrs. Johnston with a sigh. "Why, she probably had a fine house, dear friends, and a garden."

"Oh, yes! Momma grew roses and hollyhocks and morning glories." I looked over at Momma and swallowed hard. "She says friends and flowers are a lot alike. No matter how bad your troubles, they gladden your heart."

A few days later I brought Pa's dinner pail to him in the fields and sat beside him while he ate. "Pa, will you help Jim and me dig a garden today?"

Pa grunted. "A garden! Annie, I got to get crops planted first."

"But . . . we need it now."

"Don't sass me, daughter. Can't you see how much I got to do?"

"Then I'll dig it myself."

Pa snorted. "Don't think you could. The ground's too tough. It'll keep awhile longer."

But I was afraid it wouldn't.

Next morning, while Momma and the baby napped, Jim and I set to work. I chose a level spot not far from the cabin, where the morning sun would shine. We used sticks to mark out a plot.

Pa was right about one thing. The ground was hard, like it wanted to fight me. The roots of the prairie grass were like a tough, tangled web.

"Try the hatchet, Annie," suggested Jim.

I swung the hatchet into the ground and cut through the sod as best as I could. It wasn't long before my hands were red and sore and my back ached. Slowly I turned over the hard earth, opening it to the warm air.

But after a few days, our patch of dirt wasn't much bigger than a baby's blanket. "We need Pa's breaking plow," Jim said.

One night Pa came up from the field and stopped beside me. "What put it in your head to take this on right now, Annie? I'll get to it soon enough."

I jutted my chin out and looked at him hard. "Oh, Pa, don't you know?"

Pa looked toward the cabin and frowned. After a moment, he said, "Wake me a bit early in the morning, sweet pea. I'll plow some of this up for you."

MOMMA mostly slept and kept to her bed, as though something dark and heavy pressed on her. Sometimes I saw tears slip down her cheeks. She crooned to the baby but didn't give her a name.

It hurt to see her. All I could do was work.

Slowly, with Pa's help, Jim and I cleared a large patch of bare earth. Then we hoed the dirt until it was as fine as flour.

"This will be Momma's kitchen garden, Jimmy," I told him one morning. "Mrs. Johnston gave us seeds for pumpkins, beans, and peas."

"Well, are we ready to plant?" he asked.

I thought a moment. "I guess so. I wish we had some flowers, though."

Then a soft voice came from behind us. "We do."

"Momma, you got up!" Jim shouted.

Momma was standing, a little unsteady, holding the baby in her arms. She took a deep breath. "However did you get such a large plot ready?"

"Annie did it," said Jim, skipping around her.

"Jim helped, and Mrs. Johnston gave us some seeds," I said, almost afraid to look into her eyes. "Pa did a lot, too, Momma."

Momma nodded slowly. "Annie, go look in the small trunk in the cabin," she said at last. "Fetch me the bundle tied with a lavender ribbon."

When I untied the ribbon, white packets spilled out like clouds sailing across the sky. The packets looked familiar somehow.

Then I remembered. "Your friends gave you these, the morning we set out."

Momma touched each packet softly, the way you touch a rose petal. "Gifts of seeds. Here are daisies and larkspur from Rebekah."

"Morning glories from Hannah," I said. "And look! Aunt Janice gave us poppies and hollyhocks, like we had back home. Oh, please, can we plant some now?"

As I opened Aunt Janice's packet, I felt a piece of paper inside. I pulled it out and held it up for Momma to see.

She caught her breath. "A letter!"

"Aunt Janice must have written it the morning we left," I said, smoothing out the creases with my fingers. I held it out to Momma.

"You read it, Annie. I don't trust my voice."

" 'Dear sister,' " I began. " 'Don't be sad. When you plant these seeds, keep me in your heart. And remember: I will be digging in this same sweet earth, thinking of you in your new prairie home.' "

Momma took the letter from my hand.

We were quiet. There was only the wind, but now it seemed to carry Aunt Janice's voice on it.

Pa came across the field then. He held out a sack to Momma.

"I was over to see the Johnstons this morning," he said. "Victoria asked me to give you this rose cutting. She says it's from her old home and will bring us luck."

"I see I can't be abed any longer," said Momma.

She stopped, then she turned to me. "Can you hold Janice Rose a minute? I want to bury my hands in this dirt."

"Janice Rose?" asked Pa.

Momma looked around at all of us.

And then she smiled. "I thought we might call her after my sister and the prairie roses we'll grow in our new home. How does that sound?"

I reached out my arms for my little sister.

It sounded very fine indeed.